天動説前見返

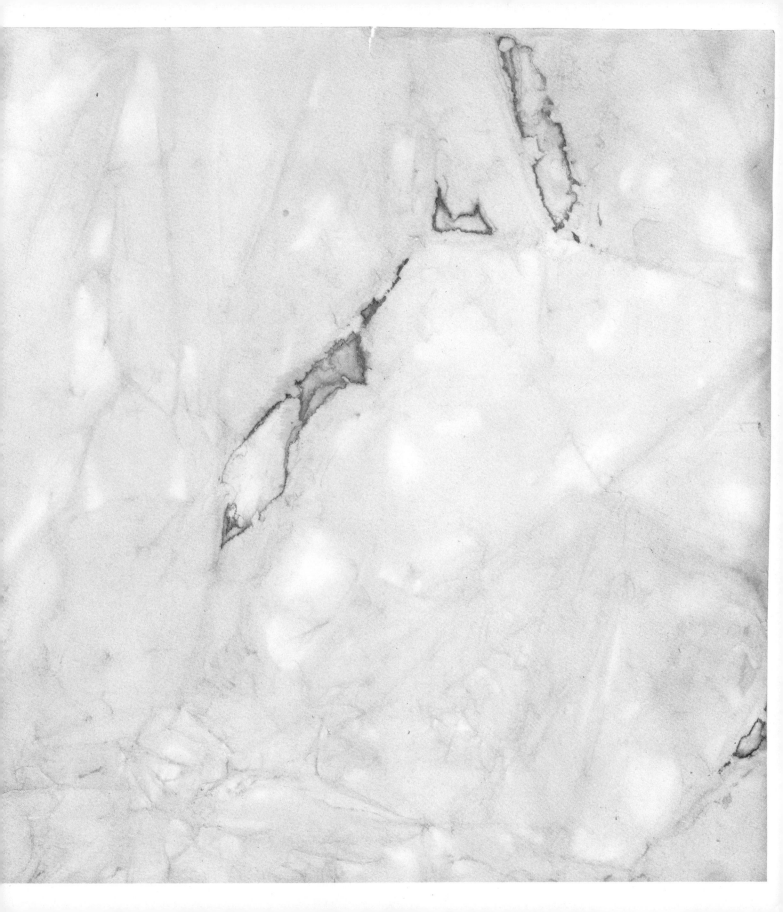

ANNO'S MEDIEVAL WORLD

Mitsumasa Anno

Adapted from the translation
by Ursula Synge

PHILOMEL BOOKS
New York

Other Picture Books by Mitsumasa Anno

Anno's Italy
The Unique World of Mitsumasa Anno
Anno's Animals
The King's Flower
(An ALA Notable Children's Book)
Anno's Journey
(An ALA Notable Children's Book)

24798

Library of Congress Cataloging in Publication Data

Anno, Mitsumasa, 1926-   Anno's Medieval world.
Translation of Kusó kōbó.   1. Civilization, Medieval—Juvenile literature.
I. Title. II. Title: Medieval world.
CB351.A4713 1980   909.07   79-28367
ISBN 0-399-20742-2   ISBN 0-399-61153-3 (GB)

The sun once shone on a small country
where the people lived by hunting,
fishing, and farming. Every evening they
turned their faces to the setting sun and
prayed that the gods would keep them
safe from all that they themselves could
not control—earthquakes, drought, and
sudden sickness.

At night they saw the moon in the sky
and could not understand why it waxed
and waned, or where it came from or
where it went. But this they did know—
that if they walked far enough, they
would reach the sea, and that if they
sailed far enough, they would reach the
edge of the world where the ocean
flowed over the rim in an endless
waterfall.

They thought that the stars sprinkling
the sky on moonless nights were like
gods watching all that was done in the
world. And if the stars could see so much
and so far, then perhaps they could also
tell what was to come. Wise men began
to study the movements of the stars, so
that they too might read the future.

When a star fell from the sky, the people expected to find it somewhere on the ground, lying like a splendid jewel to be picked up and worn. And they wondered why it was that the sun and moon never fell. The wise men were able to tell them.

"The sky is part of a huge, revolving sphere," they said, "and the stars are set in it. The sun and moon are each attached to a separate sphere, and there are many such, one above the other like layers in an onion—but transparent as glass, and all moving."

"And it is God who moves the spheres," the wise men added, putting an end to the questions.

11

In ancient times, when there were not
many schools and very few people could
read, one learned man had written, "No,
the heavens are still; it is the *earth* that
moves." But as there were no printing
presses in those days, scarcely a soul ever
heard of his idea—and no one would
have believed him anyway.

People believed that God lived in heaven and that the devil lived in hell. They believed that witches were the devil's servants, flying hither and thither through the air, plotting evil against the world.

Whenever the crops failed or the cattle died or there were floods or drought, it was obviously the work of witches. And when plague swept the land and people died like flies in the winter, it was the witches who were to blame.

15

There were no microscopes then so no one knew that bacteria existed, much less that they caused the plague. People blamed the witches for this and other misfortunes and determined to put an end to their evil—but no one really knew what a witch looked like, and so many innocent people were accused and put to death.

17

With the plague to fear, and witches, and
the devil, the world was a frightening
place. But people feared death most of
all—for death is stronger than the
strongest man.

"We must find the elixir of life," they
said, and mixed potions from the bark
of trees and from the roots of grass.
They looked for it everywhere, in the
mountains and beneath the sea, for they
hoped, by that means, to conquer death.

They knew the story about a long-ago king who had asked the gods to let everything he touched be turned to gold. The gods gave him his wish. But, without thinking, the king had touched the person he loved most in the world, and she too had turned to gold—a lifeless golden statue—so nothing but grief came of it.

That was only a fable, but many people still craved gold. Some, who were called alchemists, tried to make it for themselves. They melted mercury and lead and other secret things together in great vats, and uttered spells over them from morning till night. But not one of them was able to make gold.

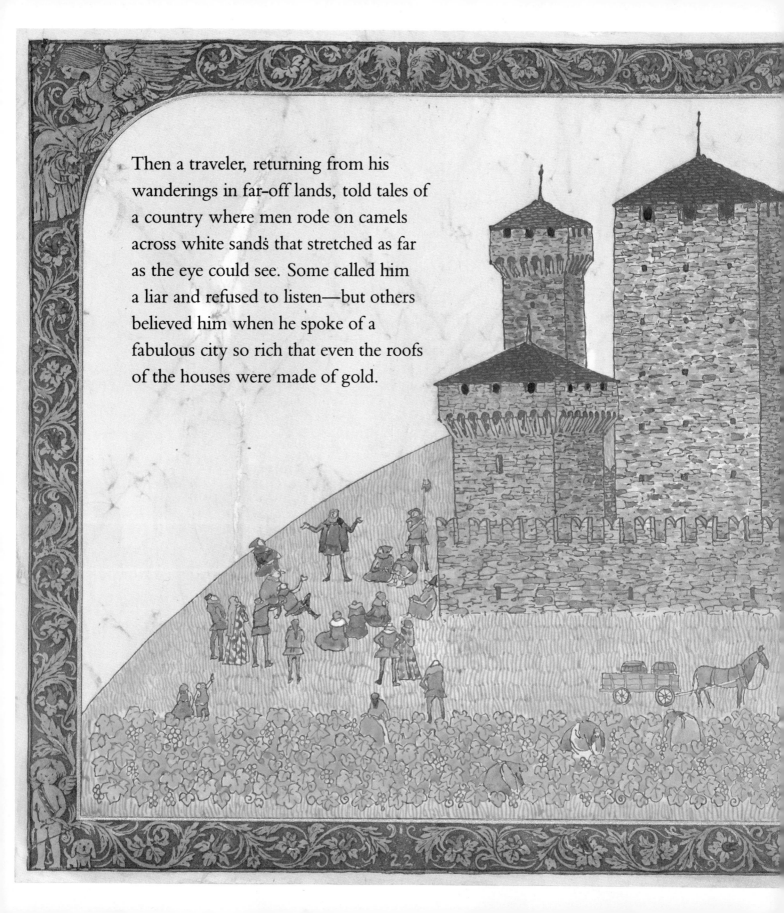

Then a traveler, returning from his wanderings in far-off lands, told tales of a country where men rode on camels across white sands that stretched as far as the eye could see. Some called him a liar and refused to listen—but others believed him when he spoke of a fabulous city so rich that even the roofs of the houses were made of gold.

23

Sailors had stranger tales to tell—and some had a bold idea. In their travels far and wide across the sea, they had noticed that when a ship approached from a long way off, the top of it was the first part to be seen. So it seemed to them as if the world must be round, like a ball, not flat like a plate—and they suggested that perhaps the golden city existed on the other side of this round world.

"The stars do not move at all; it is the earth that moves," wrote an astronomer from the north. "And furthermore, the earth *is* round."

Well, that was what the sailors had said. But if that were true, people reasoned,

then surely everything on the other side would be upside down. And if it were true that the round world turned, surely everything—people and houses, beasts and trees—would fall off into the empty air.

That was something to think about.
There was a monk who studied all that
was written about the stars, and he said,
"I agree with that astronomer. The sun
does not move at all, but the earth does.
Our earlier beliefs were entirely wrong."
And an astronomer from the south
peered through his telescope at the sky
and said, "Indeed the astronomer from

the north is right. The round earth
moves in space around the sun."
But these three were accused of leading
the people astray. The astronomer
from the north became ill and died; the
astronomer from the south was forced
to deny all he had said—and the monk,
who stood firm by his words, was
burned at the stake.

The idea did not die, however, and a
group of adventurers set out to prove
it true.
"If the world is round," they said, "it
should be possible to arrive in the east by
sailing west."

First they would reach the western islands, rich in pepper and spices, and then the countries of the east with their wealth of gold, and then by sailing still farther west, they would reach home again, thus proving that the earth was round.

Suppose that the earth was round and that the sun did *not* move across the sky, but that the earth turned continually to the east....

Then that would explain why the sun would "rise" in the east and "set" in the west as people could see that it did. Still, the idea of this great world spinning completely around every day was almost

beyond imagining. But if the older idea were true and the sun and the distant stars revolved around the earth once each day, they would have to move even faster than light, which was not possible. Therefore, it was very much more reasonable to think that it was the earth that moved.

But no matter how carefully they watched, the people could not *see* the earth's movement, and of course they could not feel it. They thought of experiments to try to find out if this new idea was true. One man had a huge pendulum made with a circle beneath it. When the pendulum was started

swinging backward and forward, its direction would change little by little of its own accord, until, after one day and one night, it had swung over all parts of the circle. This proved surely that the earth was turning around, revolving on its own axis.

But if it *was* the earth which moved and not the heavens, then the astronomer from the south had been wrongly accused, and the monk had been burned for speaking the truth. If the earth really revolved on its own axis as it moved in a great circle around the sun, then all that the people had once believed to be true was false. It was frightening to think about this.

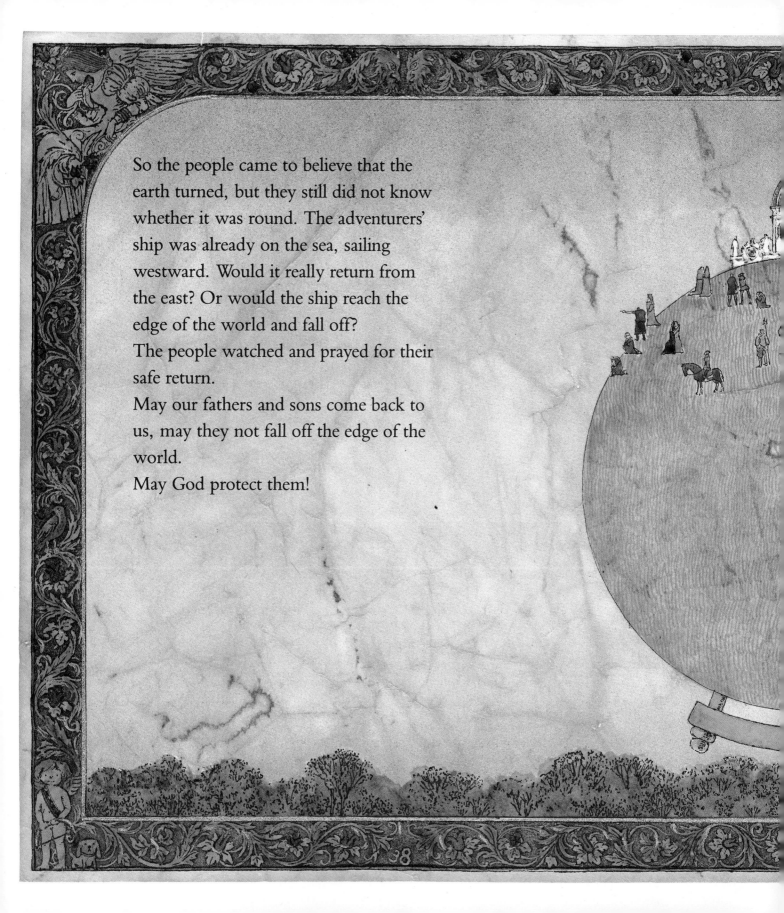

So the people came to believe that the earth turned, but they still did not know whether it was round. The adventurers' ship was already on the sea, sailing westward. Would it really return from the east? Or would the ship reach the edge of the world and fall off?
The people watched and prayed for their safe return.
May our fathers and sons come back to us, may they not fall off the edge of the world.
May God protect them!

ANNO 1970

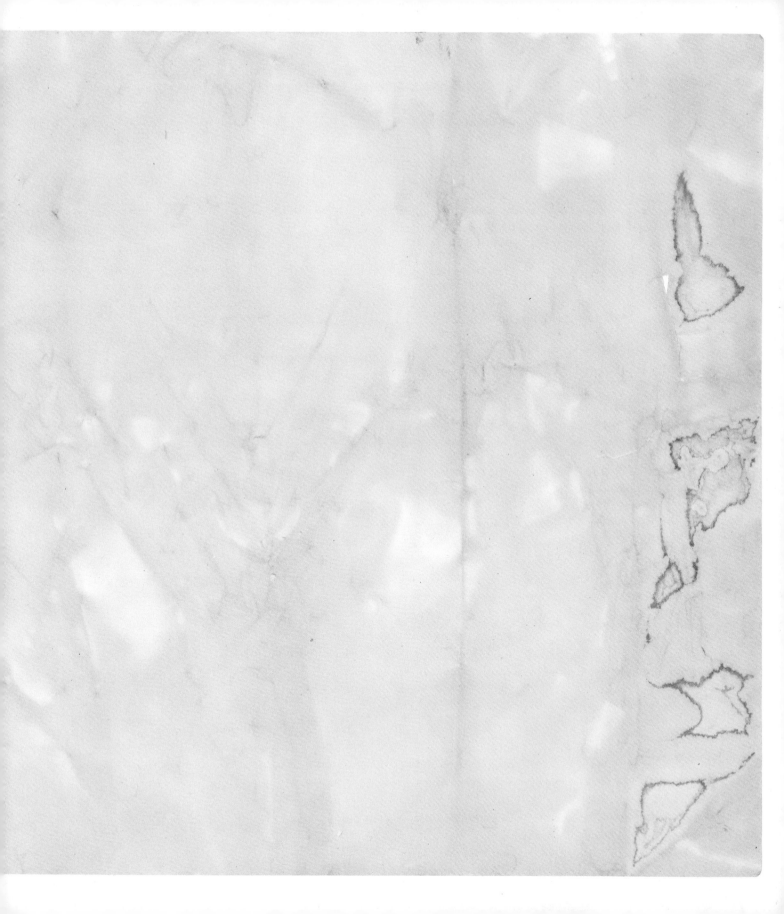

AUTHOR'S NOTE

I might have given my book a longer title; I might have called it, How People Living in the Era of the Ptolemaic Theory Saw Their World. For that is what it is about.

It is intended to show that the change from one view of the universe to another was literally an epoch-making change; with it we entered into a new scientific era from an old one which was clouded with superstition. One mode of thinking was ended and another begun.

Today it is common knowledge that the earth is round, that it is moving, and that it is the sun which is stationary—but these facts were not always known. People living in the earlier age could not understand their world as we, who look back, can understand it; they could only guess at what the earth is like. It may seem to us that they made many mistakes, but, to their very different way of thinking, these were not mistakes at all. The Ptolemaic theory stemmed from the very practical belief that the earth was motionless, with the sun traveling around it—and without the theory to work on at first we would never have been able to arrive at the (quite different) truth as we know it today. The Ptolemaic era was an essential stage in the development of our knowledge of the universe.

According to the Ptolemaic theory, the earth stands at the heart of the whole universe, which may be thought of as a huge, slowly revolving sphere. When we look at the sky, we are seeing the inner wall of the sphere with the stars and other heavenly bodies fixed in it, like jewels in their setting. The sphere moves, and the stars, being fixed, move with it. Yet the sun and the moon, as well as Venus and Mars and the other planets, are seen to change their positions every day. As they cannot be floating freely in the air, they too must be attached to other transparent spheres—and as the planets move neither in the same pattern nor at the same pace, it must be assumed that there are as many spheres as there are planets. These are the principles behind the Ptolemaic theory, and in the context of its time this theory can even be termed accurate, as it was based on the results of careful and detailed astronomical observations.

The astronomers observed the planet Saturn, and they noticed that it moved oddly—first forward, then halting for a while, then returning to its original position and then moving forward again. One of them, Apollomus, explained this curious effect as being due to its "movement which combined an epicycle and an eccentric circle," which is to say, that while the planet moved in its own small circular path, or epicycle, it was at the same time moving around the earth in a large circular path of which the earth was not the central point. Ptolemy of Alexandria used this explanation in about A.D. 130 in his *Almagest*, a vast work in thirty volumes on his theory. It is said that in order to demonstrate the complex movements of the planets he used more than eighty glass balls—and from this statement alone we can see that his conception of the universe was quite sophisticated, although he lived in an age that still believed in demons.

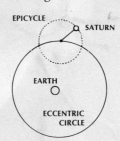

Ptolemaic explanation of the apparent movement of Saturn

Nearly fourteen centuries later the Polish scholar, Nicolaus Copernicus, when asked why the planets continued in their same courses, declared that it was because God had willed it so.

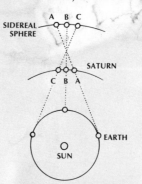

Copernican explanation of the apparent movement of Saturn

Yet it was this same Copernicus who first abandoned Ptolemy's concept of epicycle and eccentric circle, and saw the phenomenon of Saturn's apparent backward movement as being caused by the fact that the faster-moving earth overtakes and passes Saturn, as both planets orbit the sun. Elaborating his theory, Copernicus wrote a book, *Concerning the Rotation of the Heavens,* but it was not until 1543, when he was on his deathbed, that the book was ready for publication.

A monk named Giordano Bruno, a Dominican who had left his order to become an ardent supporter of the Copernican theory, went about the country teaching it to the people wherever they would listen. But at this time such ideas were considered to be contrary to the truth of the Bible and the teachings of the church—and on February 17, 1600, Bruno was burned at the stake in Rome's Campo di Fiorini Plaza. This was a terrible example of the ways in which superstition or mistaken belief have so often repressed the search for scientific truth.

In 1616 Galileo, who through a telescope had observed the movements of four satellites around Jupiter and who believed that Copernicus had been correct in his theory, was brought before a religious tribunal and accused of heresy.

We cannot now atone for the deaths of such men as Bruno, or for the treatment of Galileo, who was forced to deny his own truth and confess it to be a lie—we can only regret that such things happened in the bitter struggle between religion and science. But perhaps, if we imagine what it must have been like to be alive in those days, we may understand more clearly why the church at that time thought so narrowly and took such harsh action.

The world was greatly preoccupied with dubious and even dangerous arts—astrology, alchemy, and magic; secret charms and spells and invocations. None of the instruments necessary to a more accurate understanding of the world had been invented then. There were no microscopes so it was impossible for anyone to know that the plague, for instance, was caused by bacteria; in those days it could only be attributed to the devil....

Nearly four hundred years have passed since the monk, Bruno, was put to death—and now everyone knows that the earth rotates around the sun. Even the smallest child knows that the earth is round. This is an age in which men have traveled to the moon and returned again.

But would it be true to say that everyone *really* understands the Copernican theory?

It is necessary at this point to think about it, to distinguish between what we know and what we understand. We may "know" about the Copernican theory, that the earth is round and that it rotates among the other planets, simply because we are told that it is so; the work of discovery has been done for us.

But if it is something we truly understand, then it is no longer possible for us to hold beliefs that are based on superstition, old tales and guesses; we can no longer believe in astrology and magic. Can we then understand what it was to live in the days when those old beliefs took the place of facts?

When Copernicus made his discovery, it must have been a frightening experience for him. He knew that his world could neither accept nor understand it. Can we feel what Galileo felt, seventy years old and knowing the truth of what he said, when he had to kneel before an ignorant tribunal and swear that he had lied? Can we feel for Bruno, who stood by his beliefs and died for them?

Thinking of these men and of the suffering their knowledge brought to them and to the people of their time, it troubles me to hear it said, lightly and without any feeling, "The world is round and it moves."

For this reason I have written my book, in the hope that readers who have looked at a globe and already *know* that the earth is round, will now understand as well and feel, for this moment, at least, the bewilderment and the shock the people of the medieval world must have felt when the Copernican theory first threatened their own cherished and long-held beliefs.

—*Mitsumasa Anno*

Chronology and Notes

432 B.C. The Parthenon in Athens, Greece, was completed.

332 B.C. The city of Alexandria, Egypt, was founded by Alexander the Great. The cities of Athens and Alexandria became seats of learning, famous for such scholars as the mathematicians Pythagoras and Euclid; Archimedes, the physicist; and Aristotle, who has been called the "father of scholars." For nearly eight hundred years, throughout the Roman era until the beginning of the period we know as the Dark Ages, Greek civilization had a great influence on history. In the period before the birth of Christ, there were a number of astronomers whose contributions to science should not be ignored:

276–194 B.C. Eratosthenes of Egypt calculated the size of the earth.

About 280 B.C. Aristarchus advocated a theory of the rotation of the planets around the sun.

190–125 B.C. Hipparchus made precise and detailed observations of the heavens.

29 A.D. The crucifixion of Jesus Christ.

About 150 A.D. Ptolemy completed the *Almagest* in thirty volumes. This great work dealing with the theory that other planets orbit the earth received the support of the church and set the pattern of astronomical thought that prevailed throughout the Middle Ages.

641 The fall of Alexandria as a seat of learning. At this time the great library was burned, and the period of Greek scholarship came to a close.

Between the seventh and tenth centuries, while Europe was in the Dark Ages, Arabic culture was entering its own golden age. Papermaking and alchemy were introduced into Europe from Asia.

1096 The Crusades to liberate the Holy Land from the Saracen began.

1271 Marco Polo (1254–1324) set out on the journey to the East from which he returned in 1295. This marked the beginning of cultural exchange between East and West.

1265 Birth of Dante Alighieri. The world-view of *The Divine Comedy* was based on the Ptolemaic theory.

1348–1451 The Black Plague swept across Europe.

In the fourteenth, fifteenth, and sixteenth centuries, belief in witches was widespread. It is said that during this period at least 300,000 people were accused of witchcraft and put to death. The accusation might fall on anyone—even the mother of Johannes Kepler, the astronomer, was suspected of witchcraft.

1450 Johann Gutenberg (1400?–1468) invented the printing press.

1452 Birth of Leonardo da Vinci (d. 1519)

1453 The fall of Constantinople. This was the end of the Eastern Roman empire, resulting in the rise of the Italian cities as centers of culture and learning. The traditions of scholarship and art inherited by the Byzantines from the older Greek culture were revived; the rise of modern scientific thought was stimulated as the medieval view of nature declined. This period is called the Renaissance.

1492 Christopher Columbus sailed to the "New World."

1498 Vasco da Gama (1469–1524) sailed around the Cape of Good Hope to India.

1517 Martin Luther proposed the Reformation.

1519 Ferdinand Magellan sailed around the world.

1543 Nicolaus Copernicus (1473–1543) affirmed his theory that the earth revolved around the sun. His book, *Concerning the Rotation of the Heavens* was not ready for publication until the very end of his life.

1572 Tycho Brahe (1546–1601) discovered new stars.

1597 Johannes Kepler (1571–1630) began his study of the revolution of Mars.

1600 Giordano Bruno (1548–1600), the Dominican monk who ardently supported the Copernican theory, was burned at the stake for heresy.

1616 Galileo Galilei (1564–1642) was brought before a religious tribunal and warned to renounce his adherence to the Copernican theory, which he believed to be accurate.

1632 Galileo's *Discourse on the Heavens* was published. Again he was brought before a tribunal and this time he was forced to renounce the Copernican theory.

1642 Death of Galileo.

1642 Birth of Isaac Newton (d. 1727)

1687 Newton discovered the law of gravity, which confirmed the Copernican theory.

1835 The Pope gave permission for books by Copernicus and Galileo to be freely printed, thus giving sanction to the Copernican theory.

1851 The French physicist J.B.L. Foucault (1819–1868) concluded his famous experiment, in which he constructed a large pendulum and observed how its movement changed gradually as it swung back and forth. After a period of twenty-four hours, the pendulum had swung full circle.

1969 July 20th—the American astronauts Neil Armstrong and Edwin Aldrin were the first human beings to set foot on the moon.

The above is a chronological reference for readers of this book. The organization of the book, however, does not exactly correspond to this chronology.

About the Author

Mitsumasa Anno is known all around the world for his beautiful and imaginative picture books, designed for children but appreciated and enjoyed by adults as well. Long acknowledged as one of Japan's leading artists and book designers, his paintings have been exhibited in museums throughout the world and his books for children have won many awards and honors. Winner of the First Prize for Graphic Excellence in Books for Youth at the Bologna International Children's Book Fair and the Golden Apple Award of the Bratislava International Biennale, he has also received the Brooklyn Museum—Brooklyn Public Library Award for Art in Books for Children and First Prize in the Boston Globe—Horn Book Award for Picture Books.

Born in 1926 in Tsuwano, a small historic town in the western part of Japan, Mitsumasa Anno was graduated from the Yamaguchi Teacher Training College and worked for a time as a primary school teacher before starting his career as an artist. He has traveled extensively throughout Europe, but his home is still in Tokyo, where he lives with his wife, a son and a daughter.

ANNO
MCMLXXIX

アメリカ版
天動説後見返